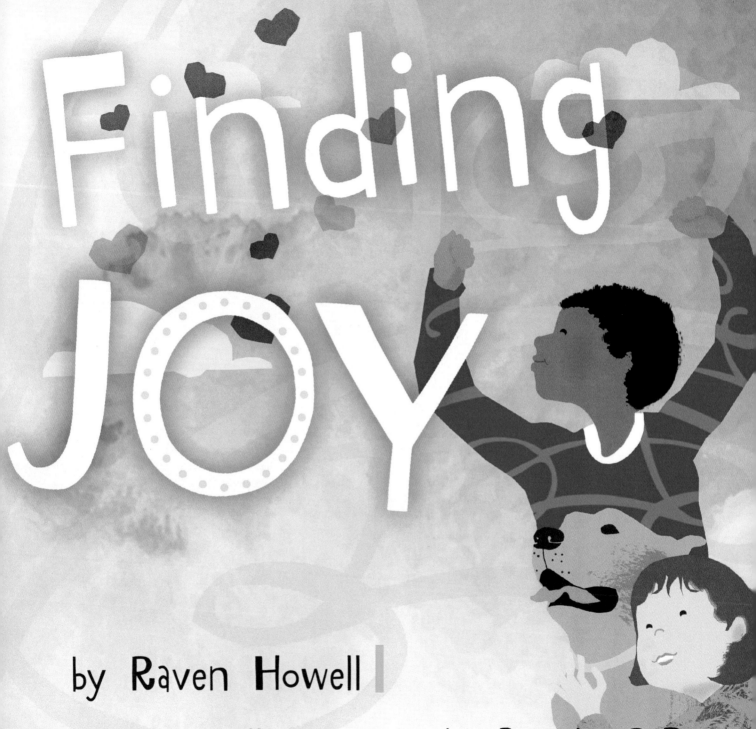

Finding Joy

by Raven Howell

illustrations by Pamela C. Rice

Linda F. Radke, Publisher
Story Monsters Press
An imprint of Story Monsters LLC
4696 W. Tyson St.
Chandler, AZ 85226
(480) 940-8182
Publisher@storymonsters.com
www.StoryMonstersPress.com

Publisher's Cataloging-In-Publication Data

Names: Howell, Raven, author. | Rice, Pamela C., 1951- illustrator.

Title: Finding Joy / by Raven Howell ; illustrations by Pamela C. Rice.

Description: Chandler, Arizona, United States : Story Monsters Press, [2022] | Interest age level: 004-009. | Includes resource guide. | Summary: A little girl and her brother are excited when they adopt an old dog named Joy. They have many adventures together, however, one day sweet Joy lays down for a nap and does not wake up. The family feels very sad, but the girl and her brother learn that it's important to remember the happy times, too. Slowly, the family's hearts begin to heal and eventually they adopt another furry friend in need of a loving home.

Identifiers: ISBN 9781589850125 (paperback) | ISBN 9781589850132 (ebook)

Subjects: LCSH: Dogs--Juvenile fiction. | Brothers and sisters--Juvenile fiction. | Death--Psychological aspects--Juvenile fiction. | Loss (Psychology)--Juvenile fiction. | Pet adoption--Juvenile fiction. | CYAC: Dogs--Fiction. | Brothers and sisters--Fiction. | Death--Psychological aspects--Fiction. | Loss (Psychology)--Fiction. | Pet adoption--Fiction.

Classification: LCC PZ7.1.H68854 Fi 2022 (print) | LCC PZ7.1.H68854 (ebook) | DDC [E]--dc23

Printed in the United States of America

Illustrations and Design: Pamela C. Rice
Proofreaders: Ruthann Meyer, Cristy Bertini
Project Manager: Patti Crane

Finding JOY

by Raven Howell

illustrations by Pamela C. Rice

STORY MONSTERS PRESS
Everything Children's Books

Chandler, Arizona, United States

My happiest day!

We adopt my brother, John.

He giggles a lot.

6

John likes eating peas.

Chomp! Mmm!

Sometimes, he gets

into trouble.

Uh-oh.

8

My second happiest day!

We adopt a friendly old dog from

the animal shelter.

Her name is Joy.

Woof!

Dad gets a bright green collar

for Joy to wear.

She likes it!

Yip, yip!

I attach a tag for the collar.

It reads J O Y.

John shares his peas with Joy.

Chomp. Chomp.

She's a happy dog.

In the mornings and afternoons, Mom, Joy, and John

walk me to and from the school bus stop.

Mom likes to sing

The wheels on the bus go 'round and 'round.

We laugh because it looks like Joy smiles.

11

During winter, John, Joy, and I

jump in the deep snow piles.

Brrr.

We build merry snow dogs!

12

14

In the spring, we splash through puddles.

Splat!

In summer months after days at camp,

we rush to Joy for big hugs.

When autumn arrives, Joy comes with us to pick apples.

She barks at the scarecrow!

Arf!

16

17

18

We celebrate John's birthday. Hooray!

We celebrate Joy's adoption birthday.

I give Joy a birthday bone as a gift.

Guess what John's present is?

Peas!

20

One rainy day, Mom comes by herself.

Her eyes are red and it looks like she has been crying.

John asks Mom where Joy is.

She takes our hands in hers.

Mom tells us Joy did not wake from her nap.

She and Dad drove Joy to the animal doctor.

The news was sad. Joy had died.

Oh!

It was hard to believe she wasn't

with us anymore.

John was quiet.

He didn't eat too many peas.

Sniff.

I cried out that it wasn't fair.

Dad blamed himself for not checking on Joy sooner

when she hadn't been waking from a long nap.

Mom though, reassures us that

no one is to blame,

and the veterinarian agrees.

After several weeks, the days grow a little brighter.

A happier Dad says, "Let's say goodbye to Joy in our own special ways."

Mom sings a pretty song.

I make a necklace from Joy's dog tag.

24

Guess what John does?

We all smile as he enjoys eating his

sweet peas again.

Yum!

Joy left John with her own gift as well.

John is inspired by Joy, and draws

beautiful pictures of her.

Scribble. Streak.

He wins a best artwork award in class.

Now he cheerfully creates beautiful

drawings of other dogs and animals, too.

Springtime brings us our new pet,

a stray cat, Miley.

Meow.

Dad pulls out Joy's green collar

he had kept and places it

on our new tabby.

Purr.

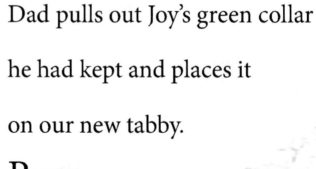

Now everyone shares a little bit of "Joy"!

27

How to Talk to Children About Loss

A Resource by Denise A. Angelo LCSW-R

In *Finding Joy*, the death of a beloved pet is told through the eyes of a child with simplicity and honest emotion. This book is an excellent vehicle for presenting the concept of death to a young child before the need for this discussion occurs.

There are many books written about death, the stages of grief, and the art of "moving on." Expert advice is of course helpful, but the difference between knowing what to do and putting that knowledge into practice can be vast. We tend to project our feelings onto our children and sometimes mistakenly assume they feel the same way we do. When a loss is suffered—whether that of a close relative, pet, or neighbor—we need to see this loss through the child's perspective and not our own. It is important to understand that we view things as an adult and that our adult view is formulated by our religious, cultural, and societal beliefs. Our children see death as it pertains to them, and questions arise:

"Grandma is gone. I want her. Is she coming back?"

"Will you die too?"

"Will I die?"

In my practice, I have found that many children worry about their parents dying and have an underlying fear, or at least concern, about their own mortality. They are often reluctant to verbalize these worries in case that might make them come true!

So how do we handle the death of a loved one with our children? First of all, give them permission to talk about the departed. We try so hard to protect our children that at times they feel they are hurting their parent in some way by talking about the deceased or expressing their own grief.

Secondly, validate their feelings. Encourage children to express their feelings—sadness, guilt, anxiety, fear, etc., in appropriate ways. Remember, unexpressed feelings may manifest themselves into anger, and behavior problems may ensue. In these cases, anger is the child's attempt to gain some control of a situation which is seemingly uncontrollable. Accept their feelings: "I know you are sad." "It is natural to feel angry about this." Telling a child not to feel sad or angry just increases frustration.

Remember, kids take their cue from their caregivers. It is ok to cry and to tell your child that you feel sad because you will miss the person who died. If you are heard expressing feelings of guilt, the child will be given the impression that there is an element of fault involved and may look for what they also did or did not do that may have caused this to happen.

So how do we help our children to work through their grief?

Make a picture frame out of cardboard or colored paper and have the child decorate it with markers or crayons. Put a picture of the person who died in the middle and hang it in a special place.

Have conversations about the good memories you both had with that person and make a memory book to write the stories in. Have the young child draw pictures to put in the book.

29

Write a story of the good things they did together so children can look at the book again and again.

Children who cannot verbalize their emotions can use play to express their feelings to you and to work through these feelings for themselves. Kinetic sand is a great medium for this type of expression when paired with small figures representing family members.

Write a letter to the person who passed away telling of how they are missed and of the good memories you have. This can be done several times over time. The letters can be put in a special box or envelope.

Play mindfulness games, such as counting the number of colored objects are in the room. Use deep breathing to calm down when feeling overwhelmed. This works best if done with a caregiver and teaches the child that we all need a little help calming down at times.

Parents sometimes ask me if they should bring a child to a funeral or wake. That depends on the child and family tradition and culture. It also depends on how comfortable the parent is at these events. A separate, private "ceremony" at home or at a favorite place can be done with young children to say good-bye and give closure.

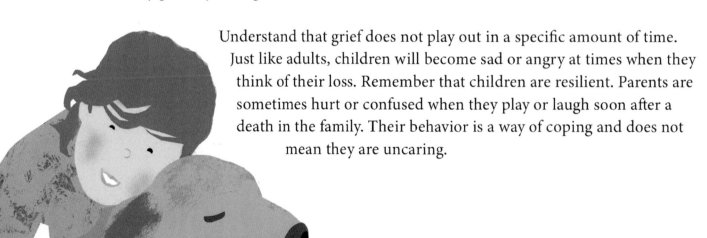

Understand that grief does not play out in a specific amount of time. Just like adults, children will become sad or angry at times when they think of their loss. Remember that children are resilient. Parents are sometimes hurt or confused when they play or laugh soon after a death in the family. Their behavior is a way of coping and does not mean they are uncaring.

30

When more support is needed, it is OK to seek help for your child. School social workers often have groups to address changing families and private clinicians can help children work through their difficulties with input from the caregiver.

Getting back to normalcy is difficult after a loss, but children as well as adults need the security of a familiar routine to move on. We can help children cope by striving to view the world through their eyes to better understand what they see as they look to us for normalcy and reassurance.

- Denise A. Angelo LCSW-R

Denise Angelo *is a licensed clinical social worker who has been in practice for over 30 years in both school and clinical settings in New York's Hudson Valley. A graduate of Columbia University School of Social Work, Angelo holds post-master's certificates in Management, Autism Spectrum Disorders, and Biofeedback. After 23 years as a middle school social worker, Angelo opened a private practice in Cold Spring, New York, specializing in the needs of children and adolescents through individual and group therapy.*

About the Author • Raven Howell

Raven Howell is a multiple-award winning author and poet of children's books. She is Creative & Publishing Advisor for Red Clover Reader, and a contributing author for Reading is Fundamental. In addition, she writes for several magazines, including *Story Monsters Ink, Ladybug, Spider, Highlights for Children, Hello, Humpty Dumpty,* and *The School Magazine.*

About the Illustrator • Pamela C. Rice

Pamela C. Rice has enjoyed a well-decorated career in advertising, graphic design, and visual communications, and now she enjoys creating children's illustrations that are fun, imaginative, and educational. Since 2015, Pam has released twelve books. including *When the Brown Bird Flies, The Painting Speaks, Aaron's Dreams,* and *Rufus Finds A Prize.*

About the Publisher • Story Monsters Press

Story Monsters Press, an imprint of Story Monsters LLC, is a publisher of children's books that offer hope, value differences, and build character. Each book also includes a curriculum guide complementing the story for parents and educators to use with young readers.

Made in the USA
Las Vegas, NV
29 January 2024

85065131R00021